WENDY THE WI‹

by

Ann Perry

Congratulations
Anabel.
Hope you enjoy.
Ann Perry x

Wendy the Wicked Witch

Copyright © Ann Perry 2022

ISBN: 9798421389156

This edition published in 2022 by
Bronwyn Editions
http://www.bronwynbooks.co.uk

Illustrated by Mr. Wolf

www.harrywhitewolf.com

Printed in Great Britain by
kdp.amazon.com

A CIP record for this book will be
available from the British library.

Dedication

For my two youngest Granddaughters,
Luana and Amara.
With my love.

Acknowledgments

Many thanks to Bronwyn Editions for editing
and publishing

To Mr. Wolf for his fantastic illustrations

To Robert Morris for his technical ability and
cover design

And, finally, to my family and friends for all
the love and support you give me.

Wendy the Wicked Witch

Whiny Wendy, the wicked witch
wondered why her nose made a twitch.
She thought about it long and hard,
then fetched her broomstick from the
yard.

Whiny Wendy, the wicked witch
wondered why her nose made a twitch.
She thought about it long and hard,
then fetched her broomstick from the
yard.

'Trusty broom, take me to town,'
ordered Wendy, with a frown.
'There's something not quite right I
fear,
so please don't dawdle. Do you hear?'

Wendy mounted her trusty "steed"
and said, 'C'mon broom, make haste and
speed.
Over hills and dales they flew,
but speeding prevented them seeing
the view.

Finally, circling the town's church steeple,
Wendy said, 'Broom, don't land by people.
There's a pet shop on the corner.
It's owned by misery guts, Harry Horner.'

'My corn is throbbing; my warts are sore.
I'm sure something's wrong inside his store.
There, I told you,' Wendy said, in shock,
and started to give the door a knock.

'Open up, you catnapper, you.
That's MY black cat. He's in plain view.
He's been gone for several days.
Ooh, you'll pay for this in so many
ways.'

'Clear off, you old crone,' yelled Misery
Guts.
My shop is closed, no ifs, no buts.'
Whiny Wendy saw red, and said,
'When I get in there, you'll wish you
were dead.'

'Ha, Ha,' laughed the misery. 'You have
no chance.'
But Wendy had started her magical
dance.
Steps to the left, a couple more to the
right.
Old Misery Guts should worry seeing
this awful sight.

Out came her wand, Wendy waved it
about.
'Wand, work your magic,' she began to
shout.
The shop window fell out, and onto the
street.
Wendy smiled... It was ever so sweet.

Next, the shop door fell off its hinges,
amidst the noise of the Misery's
whinges.
'I'm coming in,' Wendy told Harry
Horner,
and she found him cowering in the
corner.

He was gibbering and dribbling and starting to cuss.

'Shut up,' said Wendy. 'You are just an old wuss.'

She waved her wand full in his face.

Wendy was about to play her ace.

'Hickory Dickory. Hickory Hoo.

Now you will see just what I can do.

My spell will work, or I'll eat my hat.

In a moment or two you will be a cat.

But you won't be just any old moggy.

Oh no, you are going to live with a doggy.

Doggy doesn't like people, or petting, or pats.

Most of all though. HE DOESN'T LIKE CATS.'

'I'll teach you to steal MY cat.
Now then, Misery. What do YOU think
of that?
Harry begged. 'Be reasonable, witch.
Leave me alone and I won't snitch.'

'It's much too little, and much too late.
So you may as well stop your grovelling,
mate.
You stole my beautiful Inky Jack.
Now I'm going to pay you back.'

With a twitch of her eye and a flick of
her hair,
Harry Horner was no longer there.
In his place stood a cat, white and
fluffy.
Inky Jack glared, his tail, big and
puffy.

The little white cat meowed fit to
burst.
Wendy wasn't sure which was worst.
Harry's constant cries and groans.
Or the cat's ceaseless, yowling moans.

The magic wand got waved again.
Wendy said, 'My word, you're a pain.
A sniff of dust, a pinch of gnat.
There. You are now a sewer rat.'

Harry scurried from the shop.
Through the streets, he didn't stop.
Whiny Wendy knew he'd rue the day
Harry took her Inky Jack away.

Now witch and cat are a twosome again.
Together they will bring terror to
reign.
You can be sure that they'll be seen.
Especially when it's Halloween.

As for Harry, the sewer rat,
he now fears every cat.
Living in drains as black as pitch,
He regrets ever crossing Wendy the
witch.

Aunt Penny
Enjoy. x

Printed in Great Britain
by Amazon